anyt

D0602434

THE ALL NEW!

BATMAN

THE BRAVE AND THE BOLD

STONE ARCH BOOKS
a capstone imprint

STONE ARCH BOOKS™

Published in 2015 by Stone Arch Books
A Capstone Imprint
1710 Roe Crest Drive
North Mankato, MN 56003
www.capstonepub.com

Originally published by DC Comics in the U.S. in single magazine form as The All-New Batman: The Brave and the Bold #5.
Original U.S. Editor: Jim Chadwick

DC Comics
1700 Broadway, New York, NY 10019
A Warner Bros. Entertainment Company

Library of Congress Cataloging-in-Publication Data

Fisch, Sholly, author.
Manhandled by manhunters! / Sholly Fisch, writer ; Rick Burchett, penciller ; Dan Davis, inker ; Gabe Eltaeb, colorist.
pages cm. -- (The all-new Batman: the brave and the bold ; 5)
"Originally published by DC Comics in the U.S. in single magazine form as The All-New Batman: The Brave and the Bold #5."
"Batman created by Bob Kane."
Summary: Accused of stealing a sacred gem, Lenni is chased to Earth by the Manhunters and it is up to Batman and the Green Lantern to help him find Lobo, the real culprit.
ISBN 978-1-4342-9662-7 (library binding)
1. Batman (Fictitious character)--Comic books, strips, etc. 2. Batman (Fictitious character)--Juvenile fiction. 3. Green Lantern (Fictitious character)--Comic books, strips, etc. 4. Green Lantern (Fictitious character)--Juvenile fiction. 5. Superheroes--Comic books, strips, etc. 6. Superheroes--Juvenile fiction. 7. Robots--Comic books, strips, etc. 8. Robots--Juvenile fiction. 9. Graphic novels. (1. Graphic novels. 2. Superheroes--Fiction. 3. Robots--Fiction.) I. Burchett, Rick, illustrator. II. Kane, Bob, creator. III. Title.

PZ7.7.F57Man 2015
741.5'973--dc23

2014028254

STONE ARCH BOOKS
Ashley C. Andersen Zantop Publisher
Michael Dahl Editorial Director
Eliza Leahy Editor
Heather Kindseth Creative Director
Bob Lentz Art Director
Peggie Carley Designer
Katy LaVigne Production Specialist

Printed in China by Nordica.
0914/CA21401510
092014 008470NORDS15

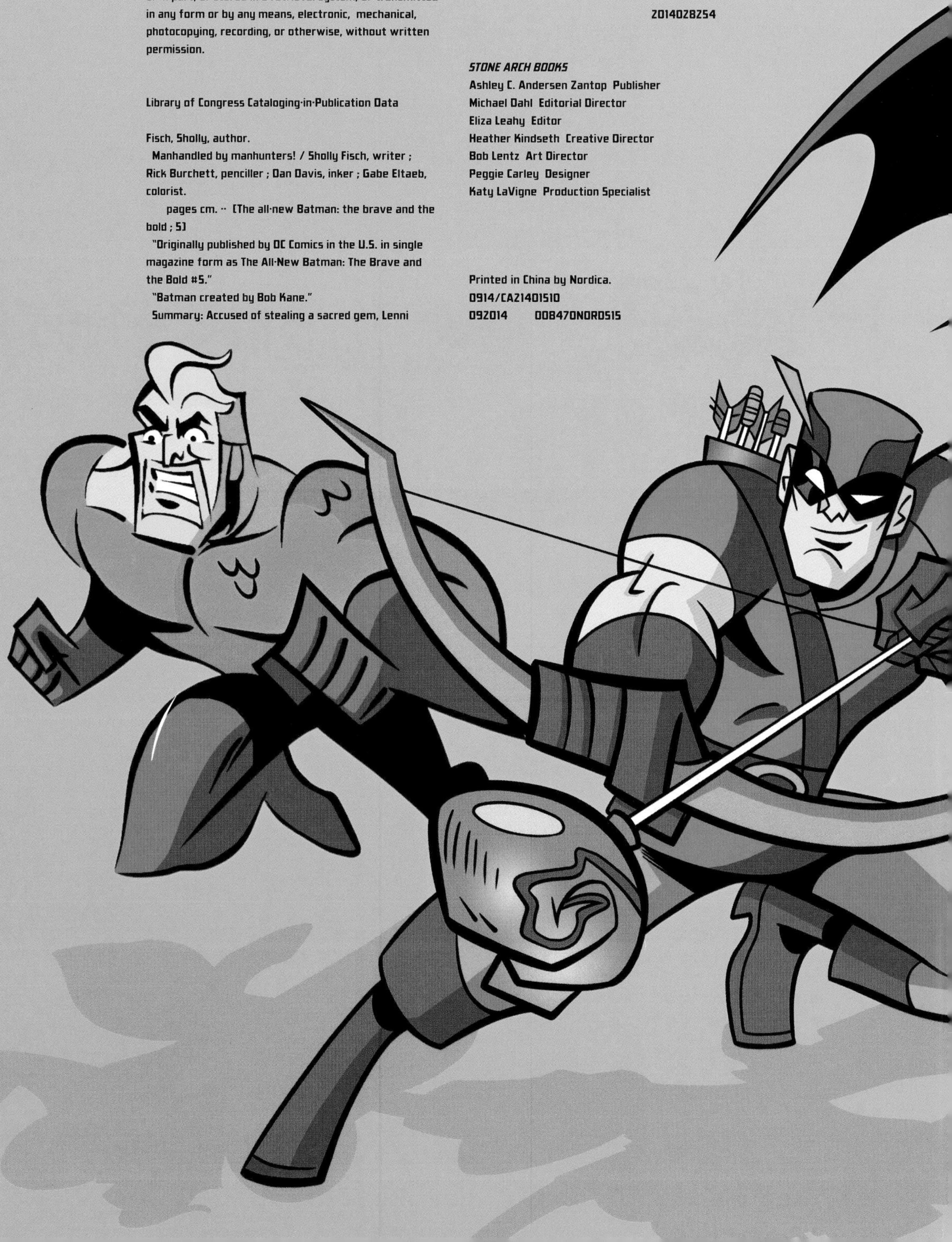

THE ALL NEW!

BATMAN
THE BRAVE AND THE BOLD

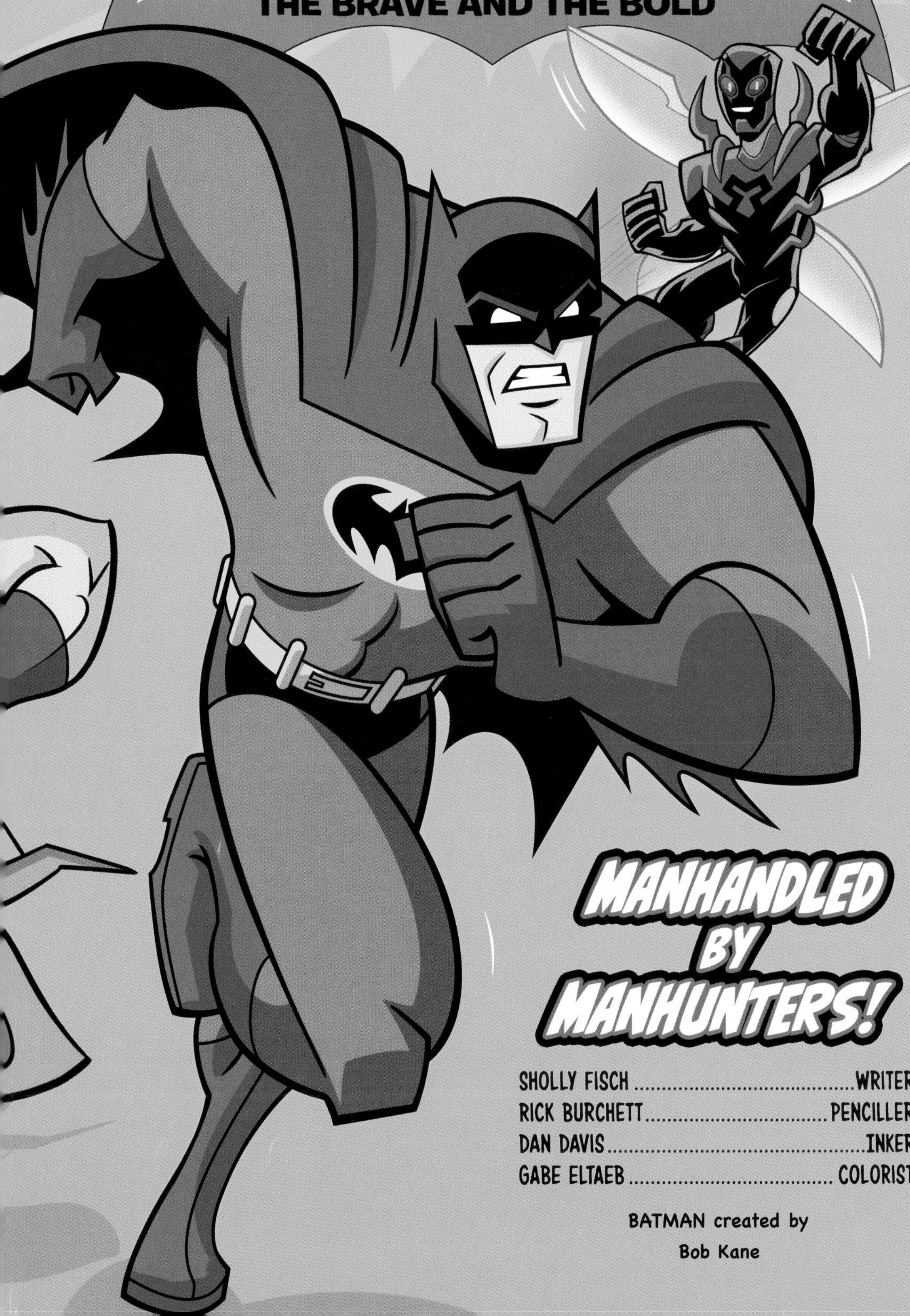

MANHANDLED BY MANHUNTERS!

SHOLLY FISCH .... WRITER
RICK BURCHETT .... PENCILLER
DAN DAVIS .... INKER
GABE ELTAEB .... COLORIST

BATMAN created by
Bob Kane

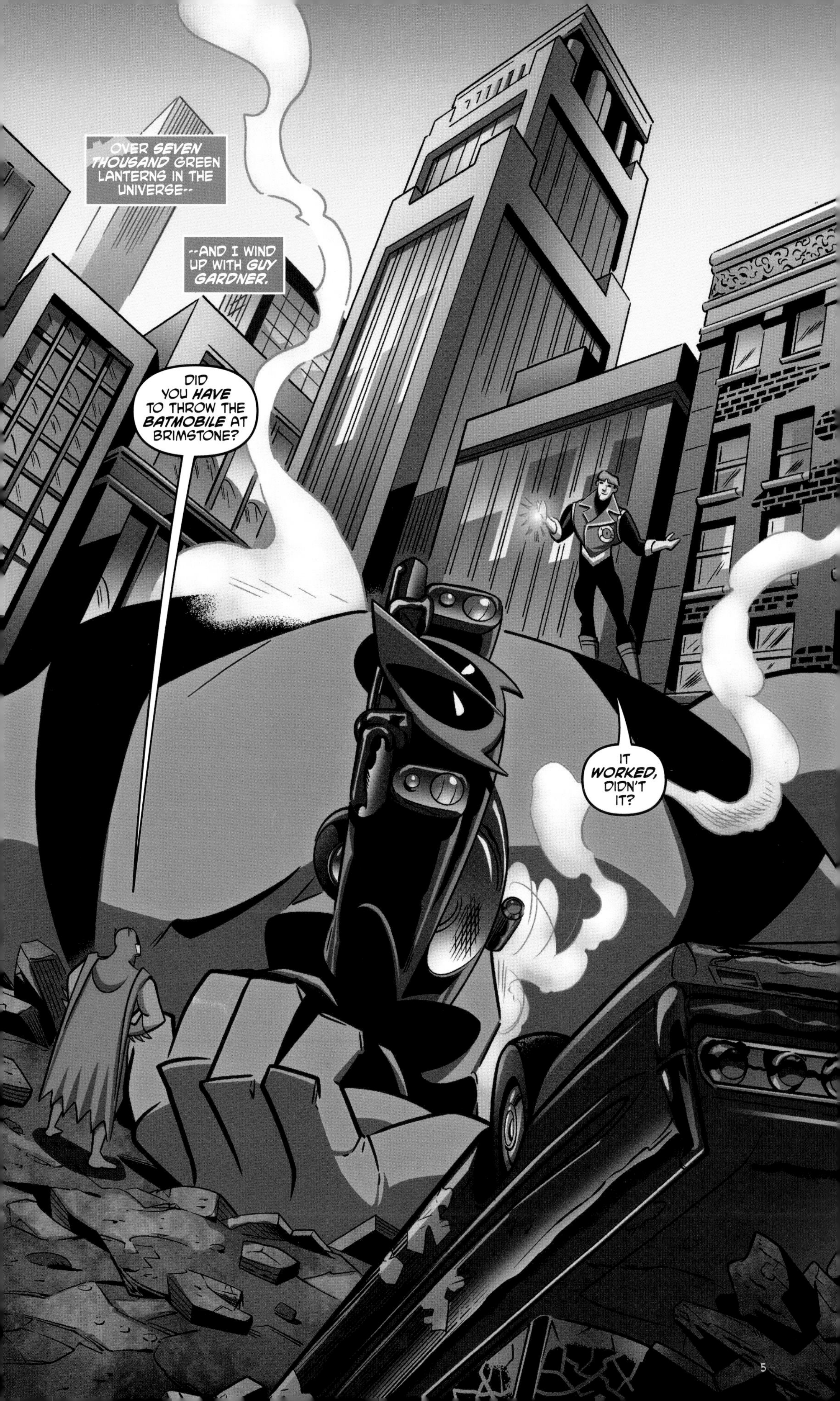
OVER SEVEN THOUSAND GREEN LANTERNS IN THE UNIVERSE--
--AND I WIND UP WITH GUY GARDNER.
DID YOU HAVE TO THROW THE BATMOBILE AT BRIMSTONE?
IT WORKED, DIDN'T IT?

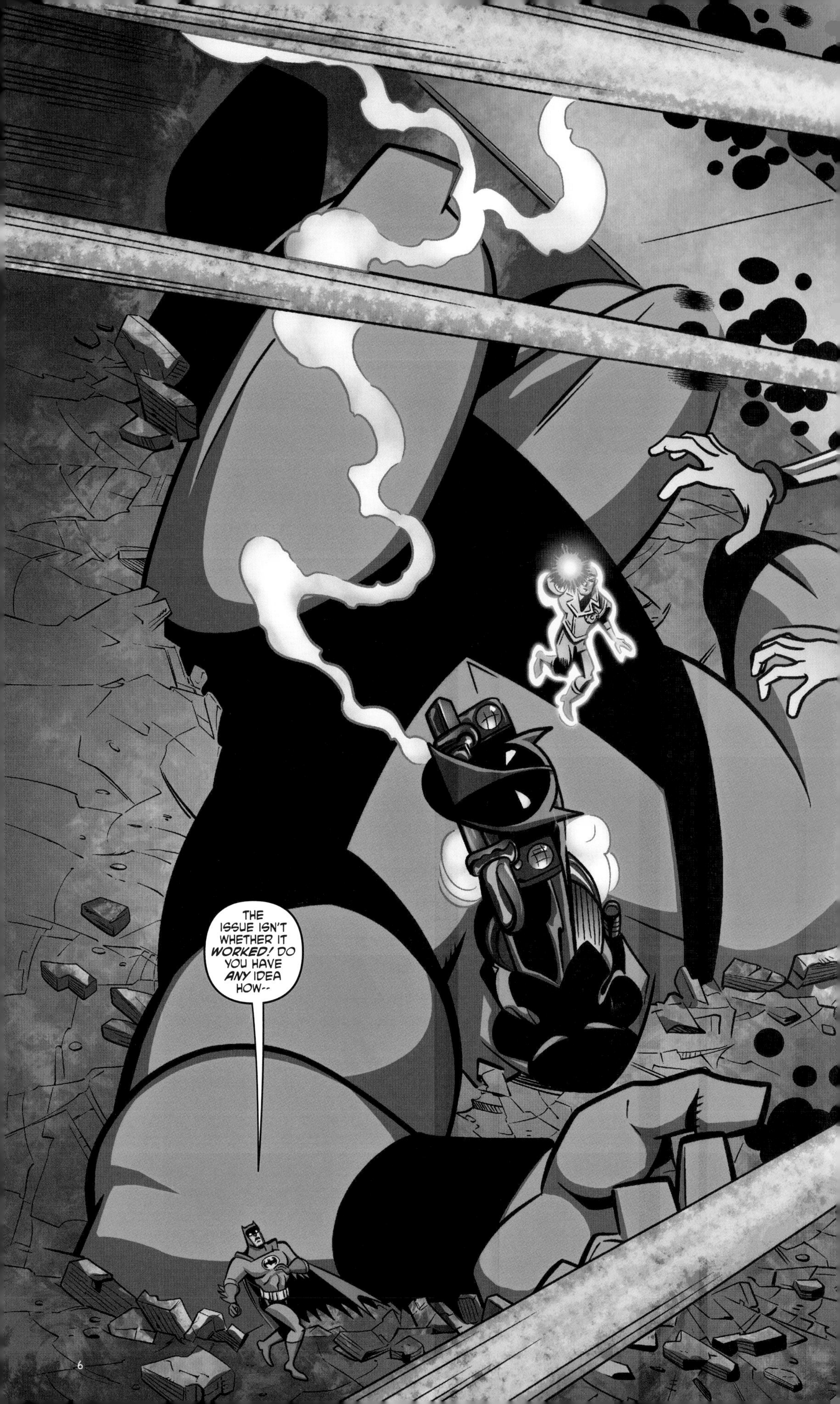
THE ISSUE ISN'T WHETHER IT WORKED! DO YOU HAVE ANY IDEA HOW--

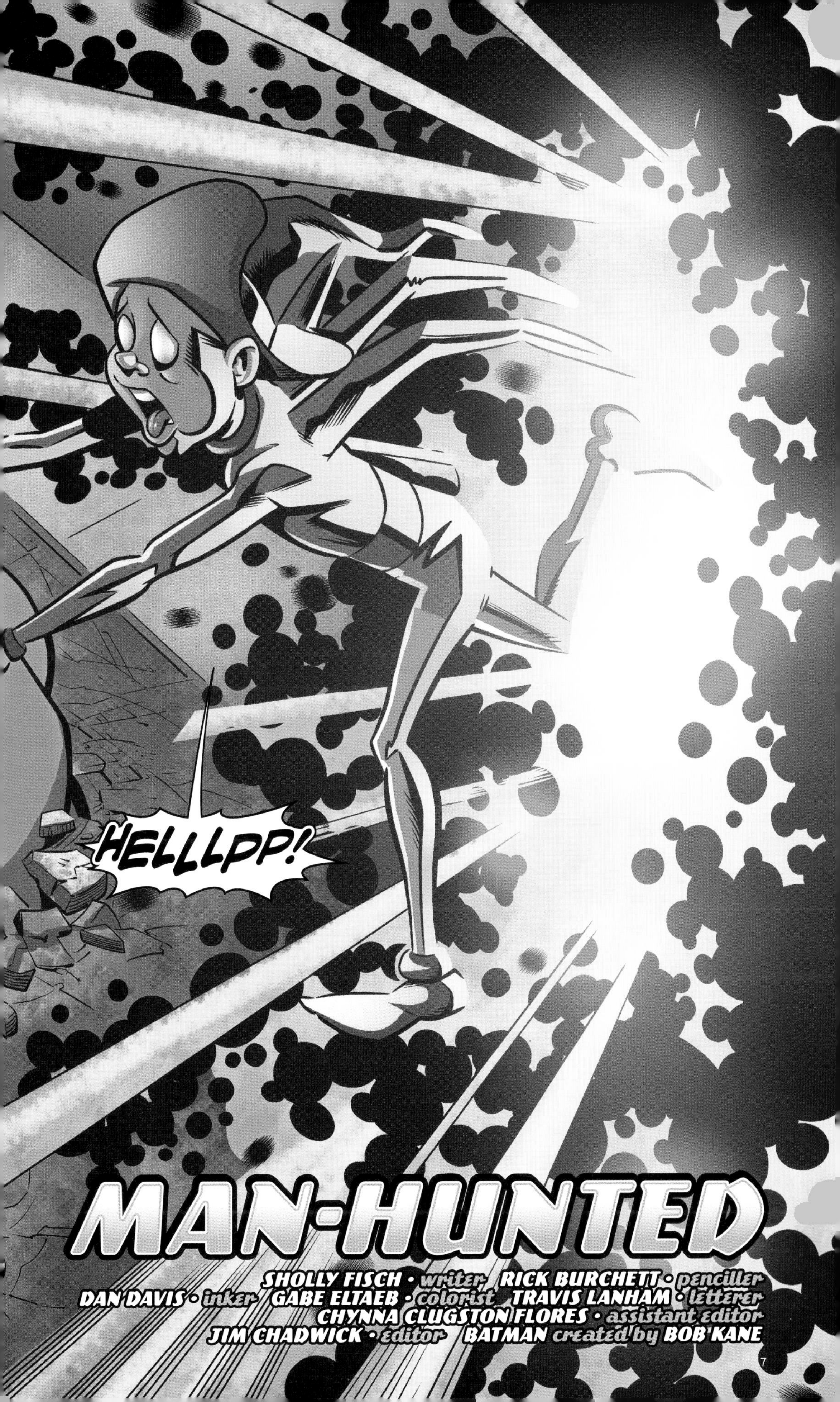
HELLLPP!
MAN-HUNTED
SHOLLY FISCH • writer RICK BURCHETT • penciller
DAN DAVIS • inker GABE ELTAEB • colorist TRAVIS LANHAM • letterer
CHYNNA CLUGSTON FLORES • assistant editor
JIM CHADWICK • editor BATMAN created by BOB KANE

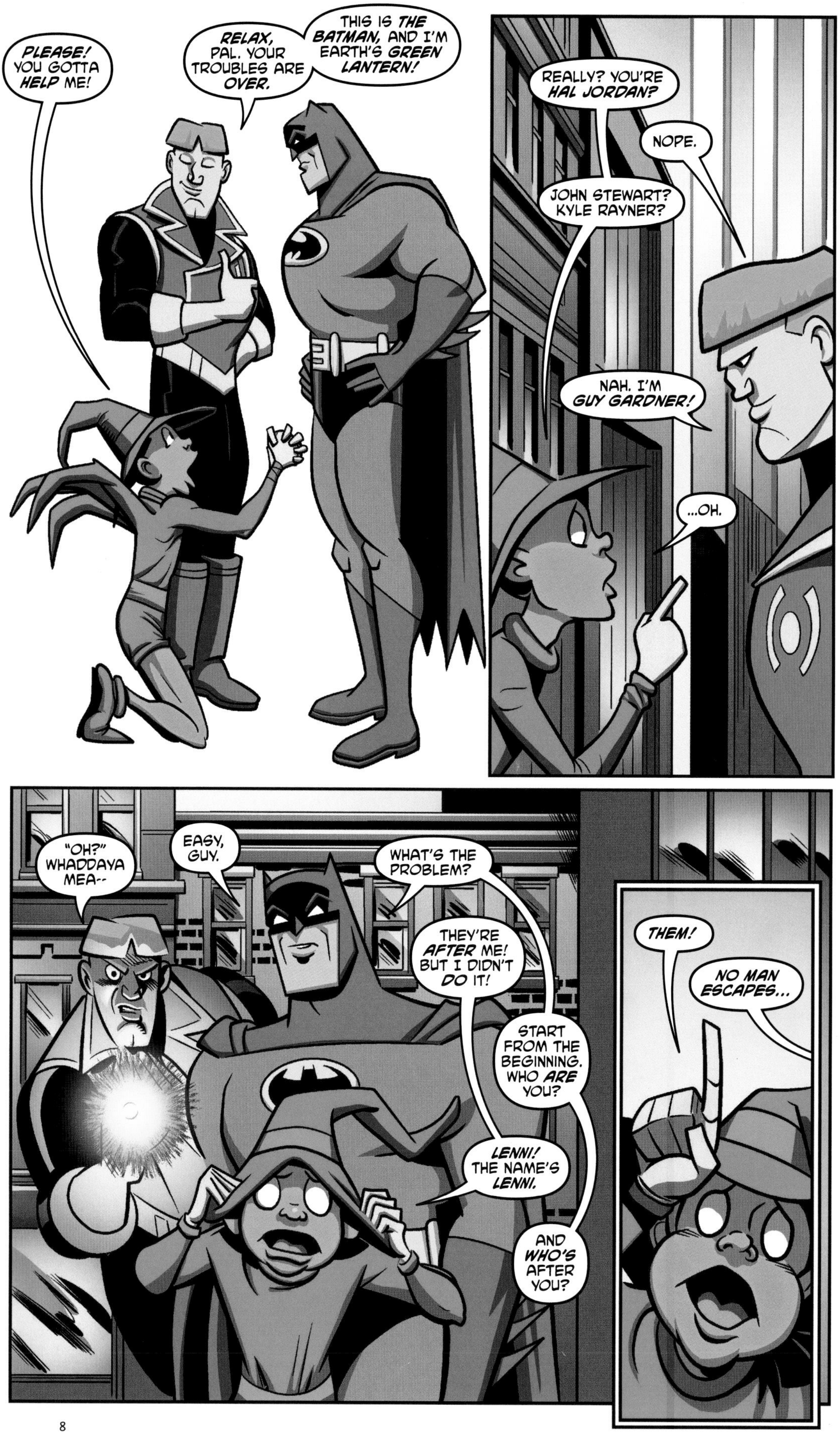

PLEASE! YOU GOTTA HELP ME!
RELAX, PAL. YOUR TROUBLES ARE OVER.
THIS IS THE BATMAN, AND I'M EARTH'S GREEN LANTERN!
REALLY? YOU'RE HAL JORDAN?
NOPE.
JOHN STEWART? KYLE RAYNER?
NAH. I'M GUY GARDNER!
...OH.
"OH?" WHADDAYA MEA--
EASY, GUY.
WHAT'S THE PROBLEM?
THEY'RE AFTER ME! BUT I DIDN'T DO IT!
START FROM THE BEGINNING. WHO ARE YOU?
LENNI! THE NAME'S LENNI.
AND WHO'S AFTER YOU?
THEM!
NO MAN ESCAPES...

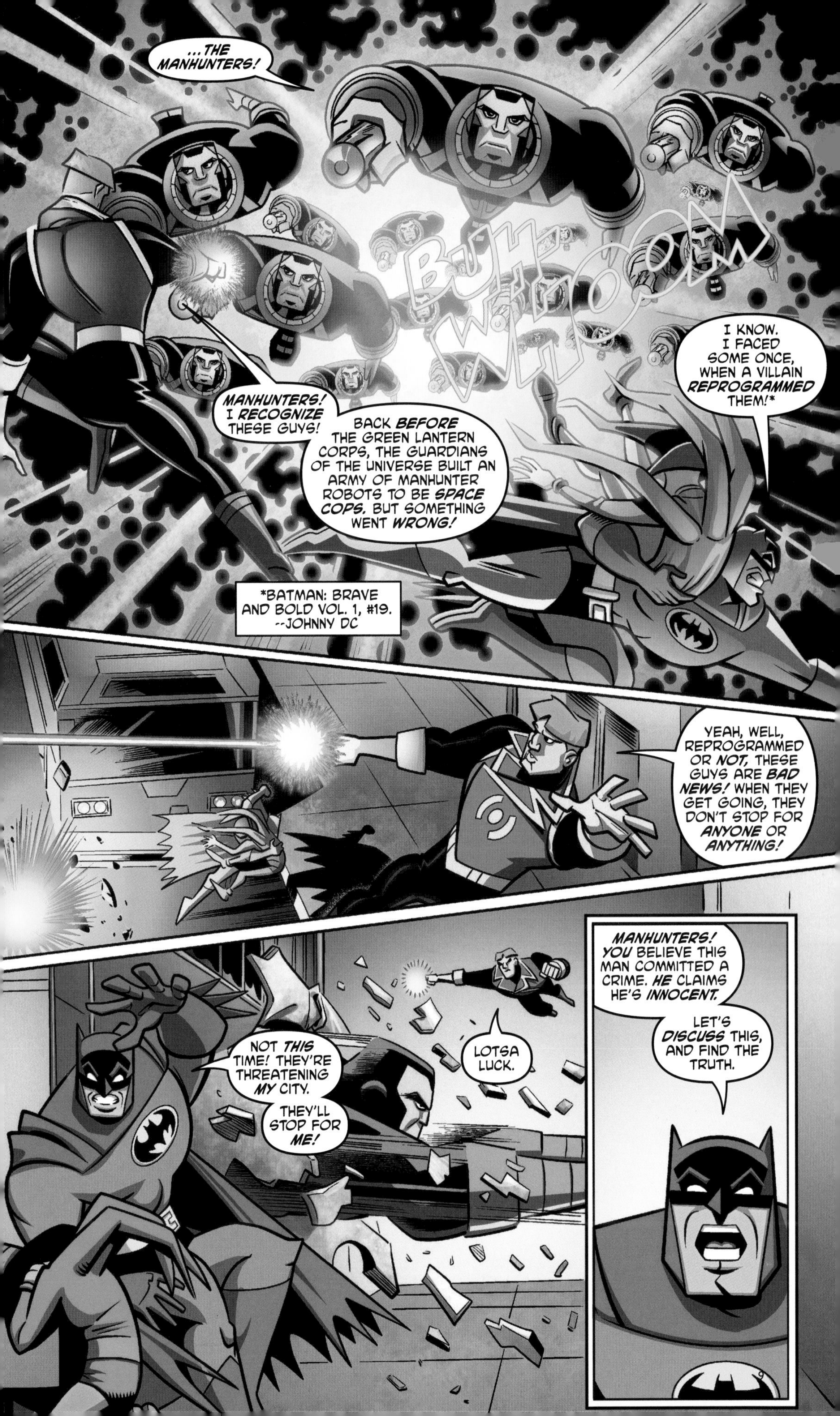
...THE MANHUNTERS!
BUH-WHOOM
MANHUNTERS! I RECOGNIZE THESE GUYS!
BACK BEFORE THE GREEN LANTERN CORPS, THE GUARDIANS OF THE UNIVERSE BUILT AN ARMY OF MANHUNTER ROBOTS TO BE SPACE COPS. BUT SOMETHING WENT WRONG!
I KNOW. I FACED SOME ONCE, WHEN A VILLAIN REPROGRAMMED THEM!*
*BATMAN: BRAVE AND BOLD VOL. 1, #19. --JOHNNY DC
YEAH, WELL, REPROGRAMMED OR NOT, THESE GUYS ARE BAD NEWS! WHEN THEY GET GOING, THEY DON'T STOP FOR ANYONE OR ANYTHING!
NOT THIS TIME! THEY'RE THREATENING MY CITY.
THEY'LL STOP FOR ME!
LOTSA LUCK.
MANHUNTERS! YOU BELIEVE THIS MAN COMMITTED A CRIME. HE CLAIMS HE'S INNOCENT.
LET'S DISCUSS THIS, AND FIND THE TRUTH.
9

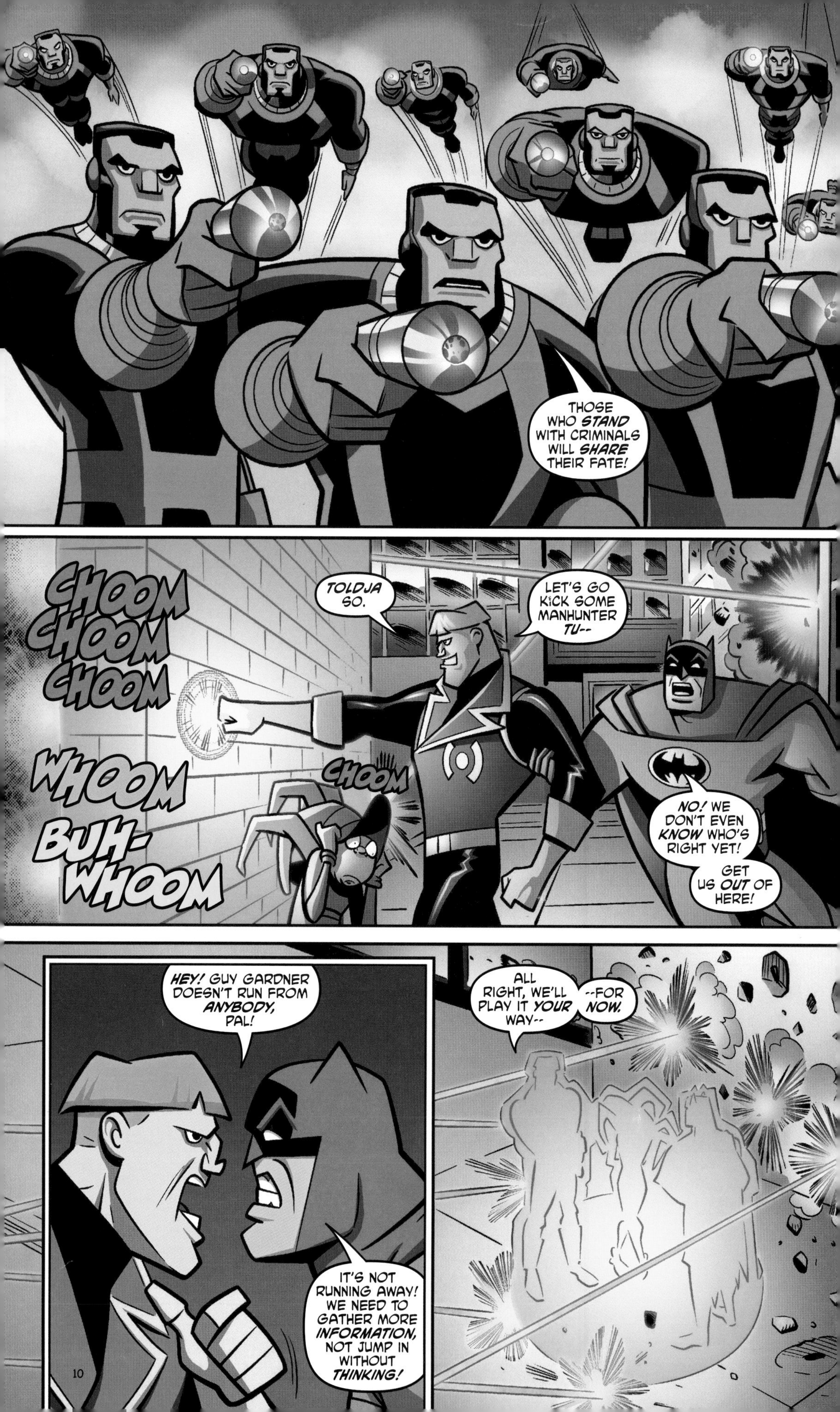
THOSE WHO STAND WITH CRIMINALS WILL SHARE THEIR FATE!
CHOOM CHOOM CHOOM
WHOOM
BUH-WHOOM
TOLDJA SO.
LET'S GO KICK SOME MANHUNTER TU--
CHOOM
NO! WE DON'T EVEN KNOW WHO'S RIGHT YET!
GET US OUT OF HERE!
HEY! GUY GARDNER DOESN'T RUN FROM ANYBODY, PAL!
IT'S NOT RUNNING AWAY! WE NEED TO GATHER MORE INFORMATION, NOT JUMP IN WITHOUT THINKING!
ALL RIGHT, WE'LL PLAY IT YOUR WAY--
--FOR NOW.

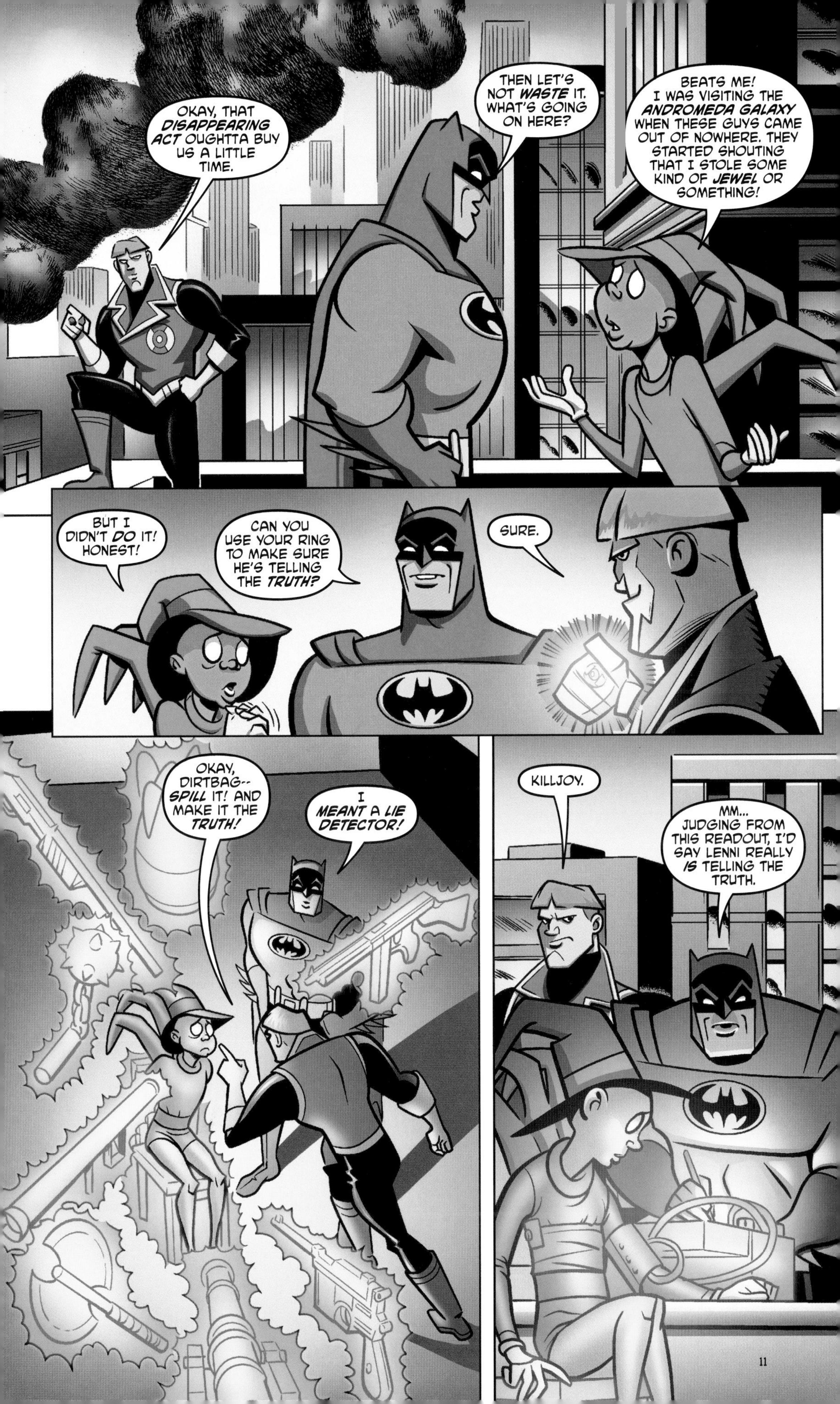
OKAY, THAT DISAPPEARING ACT OUGHTTA BUY US A LITTLE TIME.
THEN LET'S NOT WASTE IT. WHAT'S GOING ON HERE?
BEATS ME! I WAS VISITING THE ANDROMEDA GALAXY WHEN THESE GUYS CAME OUT OF NOWHERE. THEY STARTED SHOUTING THAT I STOLE SOME KIND OF JEWEL OR SOMETHING!
BUT I DIDN'T DO IT! HONEST!
CAN YOU USE YOUR RING TO MAKE SURE HE'S TELLING THE TRUTH?
SURE.
OKAY, DIRTBAG-- SPILL IT! AND MAKE IT THE TRUTH!
I MEANT A LIE DETECTOR!
KILLJOY.
MM... JUDGING FROM THIS READOUT, I'D SAY LENNI REALLY IS TELLING THE TRUTH.

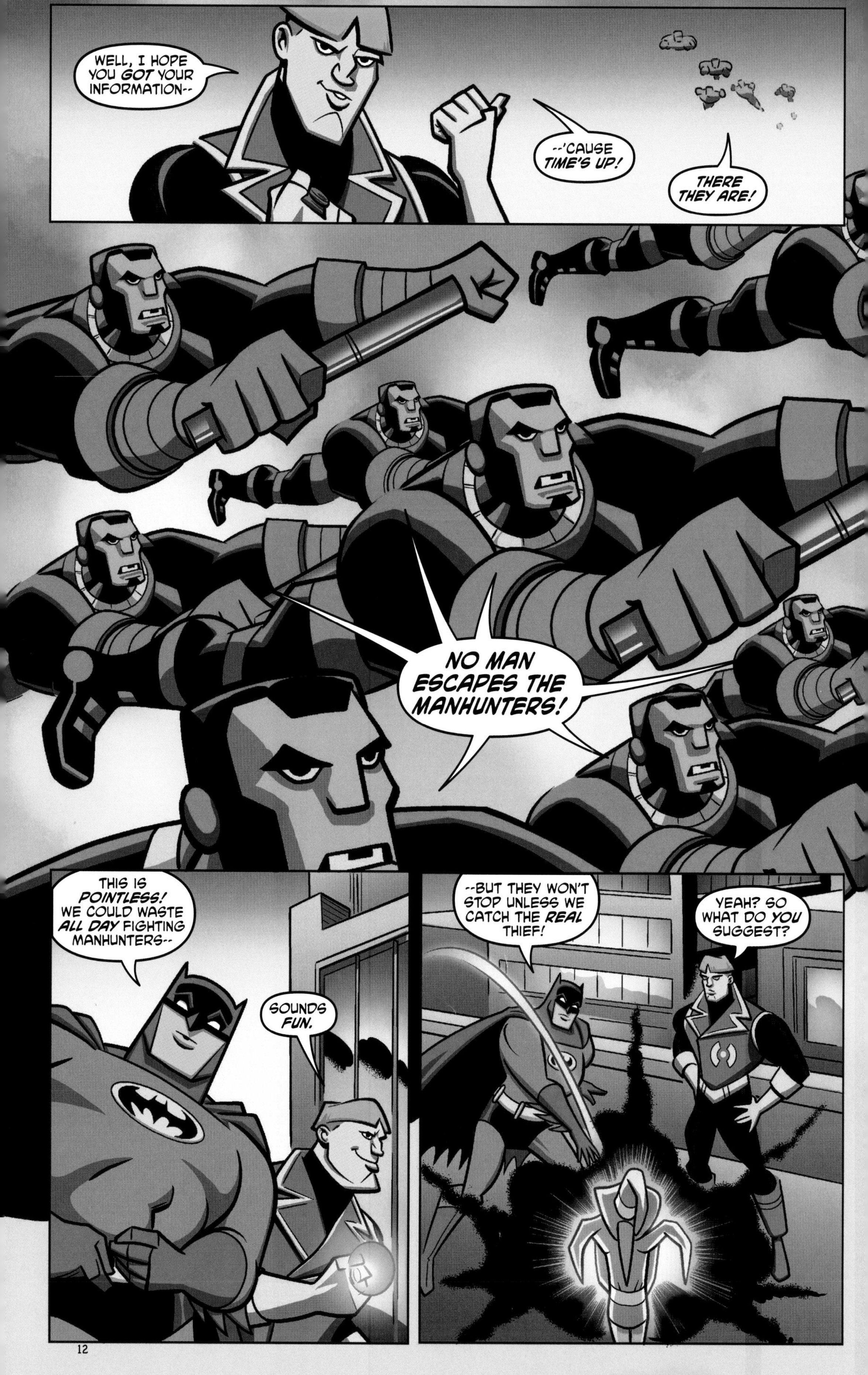
WELL, I HOPE YOU GOT YOUR INFORMATION--
--'CAUSE TIME'S UP!
THERE THEY ARE!
NO MAN ESCAPES THE MANHUNTERS!
THIS IS POINTLESS! WE COULD WASTE ALL DAY FIGHTING MANHUNTERS--
SOUNDS FUN.
--BUT THEY WON'T STOP UNLESS WE CATCH THE REAL THIEF!
YEAH? SO WHAT DO YOU SUGGEST?

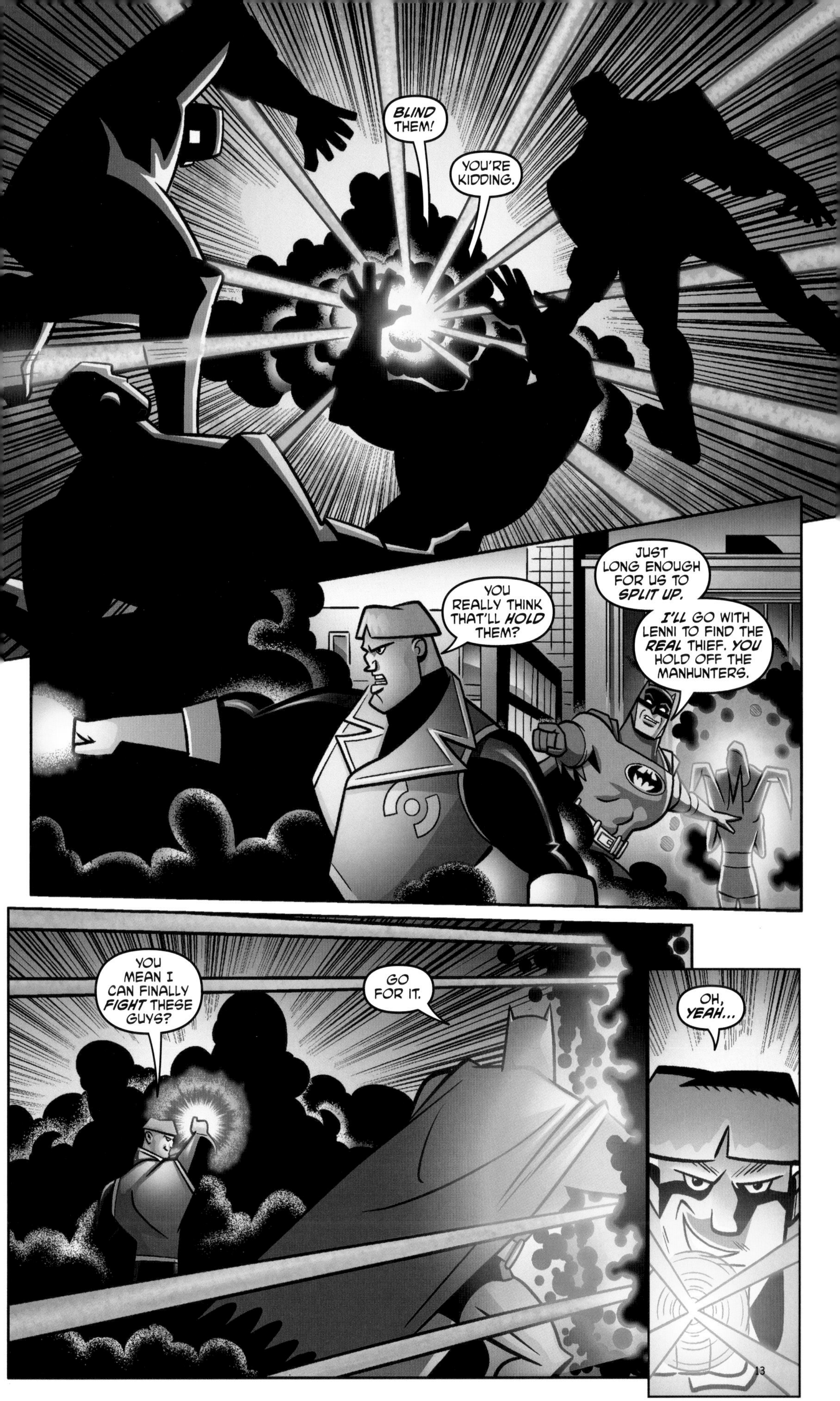

BLIND THEM!
YOU'RE KIDDING.
YOU REALLY THINK THAT'LL HOLD THEM?
JUST LONG ENOUGH FOR US TO SPLIT UP.
I'LL GO WITH LENNI TO FIND THE REAL THIEF. YOU HOLD OFF THE MANHUNTERS.
YOU MEAN I CAN FINALLY FIGHT THESE GUYS?
GO FOR IT.
OH, YEAH...

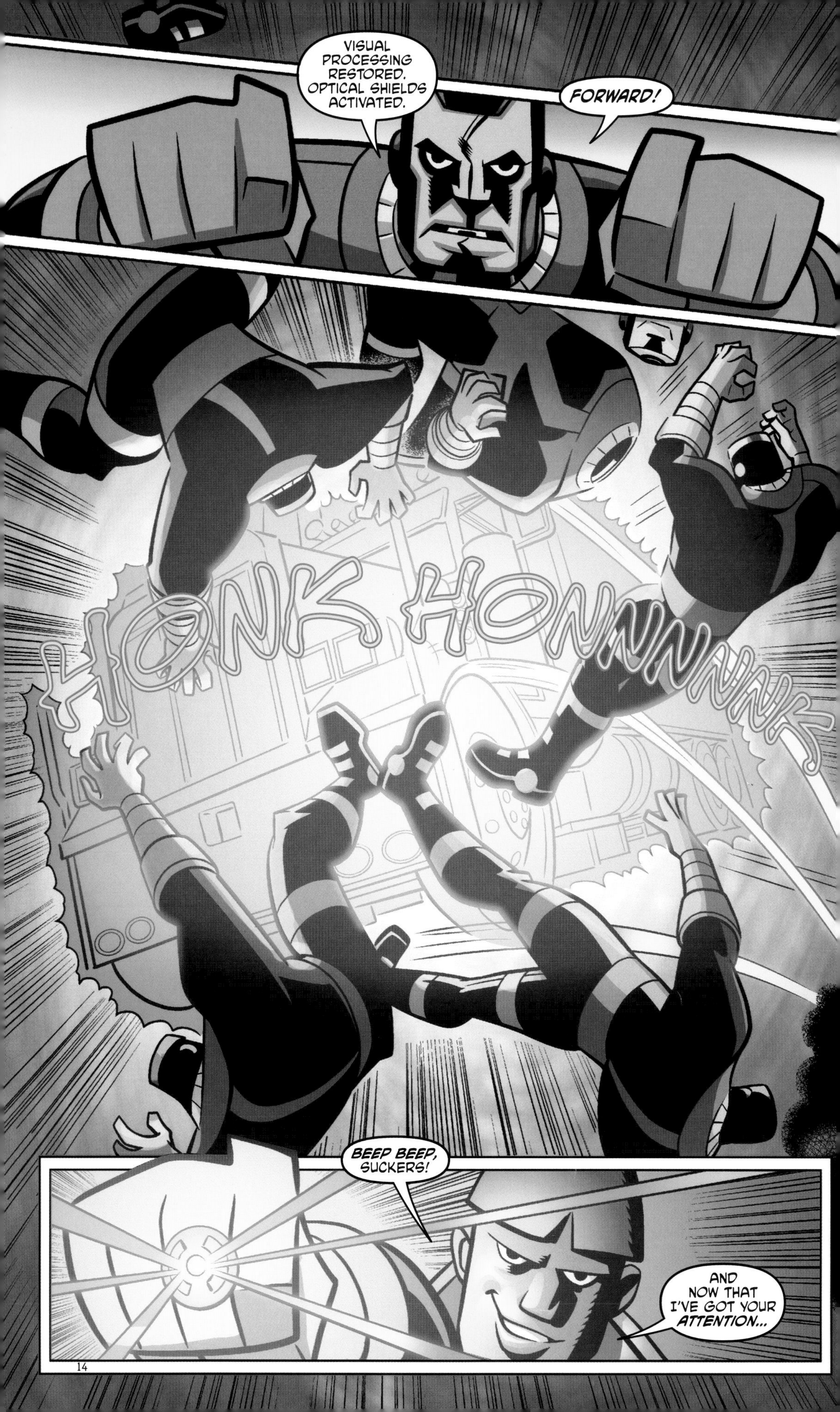
VISUAL PROCESSING RESTORED. OPTICAL SHIELDS ACTIVATED.
FORWARD!
HONK HONNNNNNK
BEEP BEEP, SUCKERS!
AND NOW THAT I'VE GOT YOUR ATTENTION...

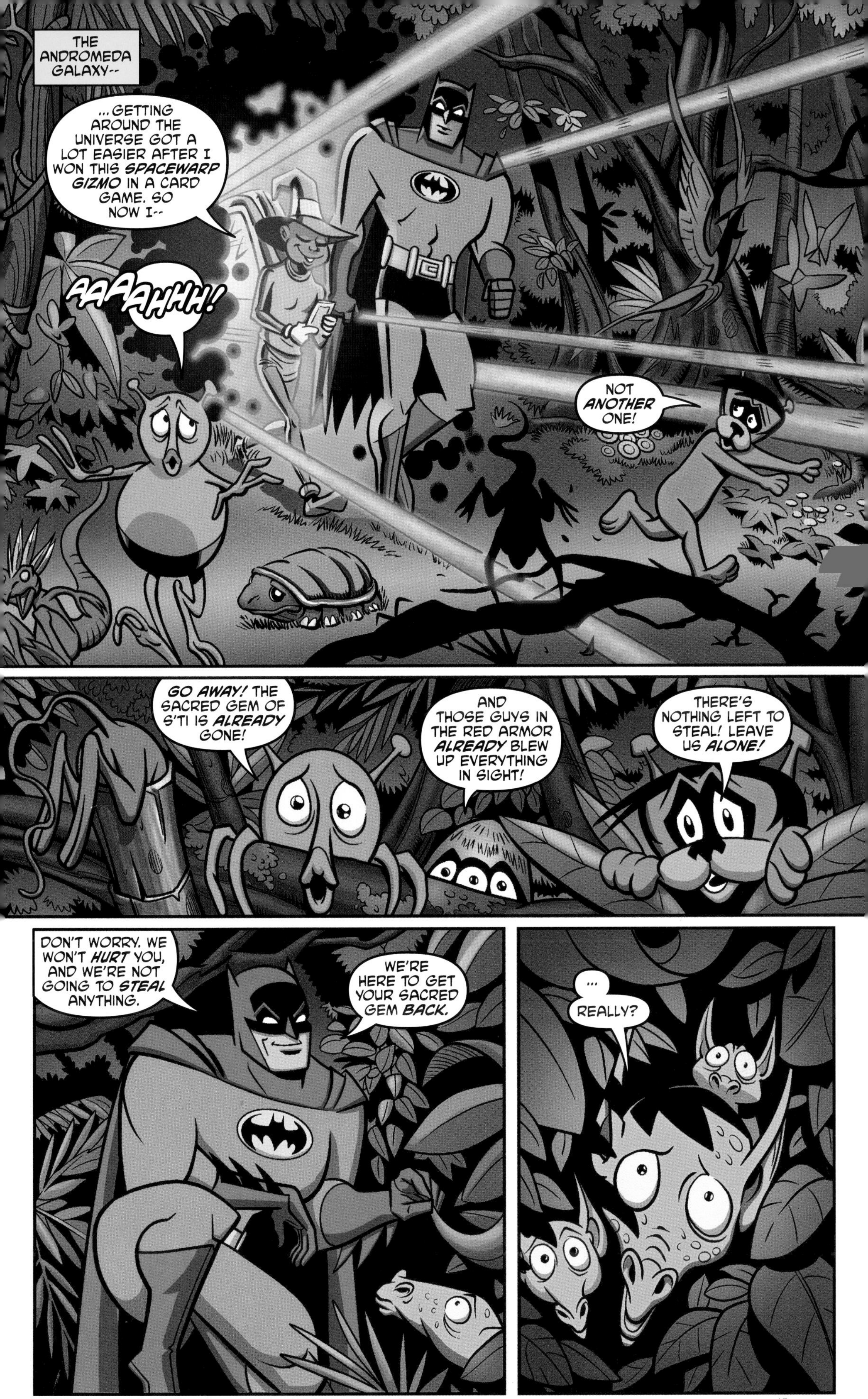
THE ANDROMEDA GALAXY--
...GETTING AROUND THE UNIVERSE GOT A LOT EASIER AFTER I WON THIS SPACEWARP GIZMO IN A CARD GAME. SO NOW I--
AAAAHHH!
NOT ANOTHER ONE!
GO AWAY! THE SACRED GEM OF S'TI IS ALREADY GONE!
AND THOSE GUYS IN THE RED ARMOR ALREADY BLEW UP EVERYTHING IN SIGHT!
THERE'S NOTHING LEFT TO STEAL! LEAVE US ALONE!
DON'T WORRY. WE WON'T HURT YOU, AND WE'RE NOT GOING TO STEAL ANYTHING.
WE'RE HERE TO GET YOUR SACRED GEM BACK.
...
REALLY?

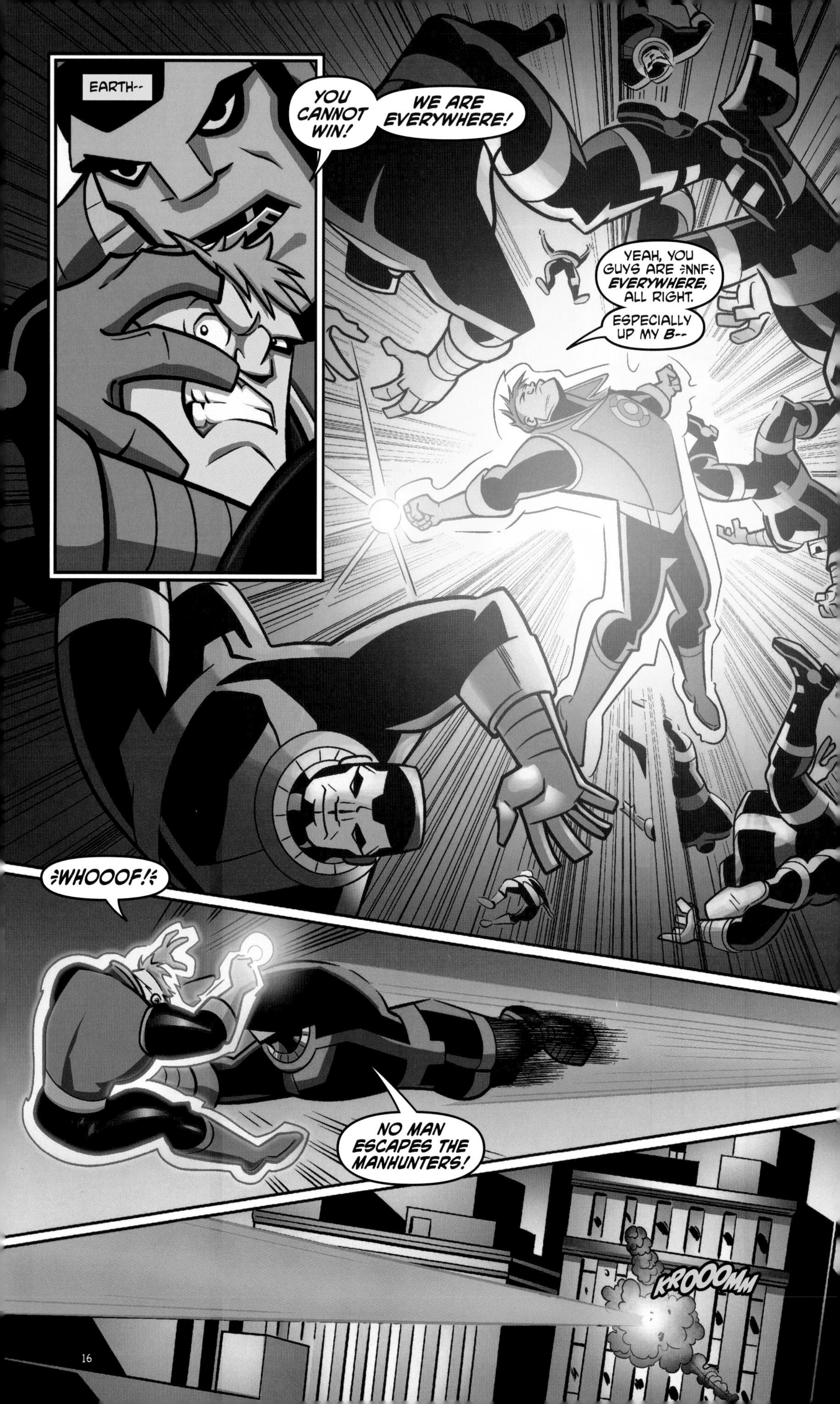
EARTH--
YOU CANNOT WIN!
WE ARE EVERYWHERE!
YEAH, YOU GUYS ARE ⁖NNF⁖ EVERYWHERE, ALL RIGHT.
ESPECIALLY UP MY B--
⁖WHOOOF!⁖
NO MAN ESCAPES THE MANHUNTERS!
KROOOMM

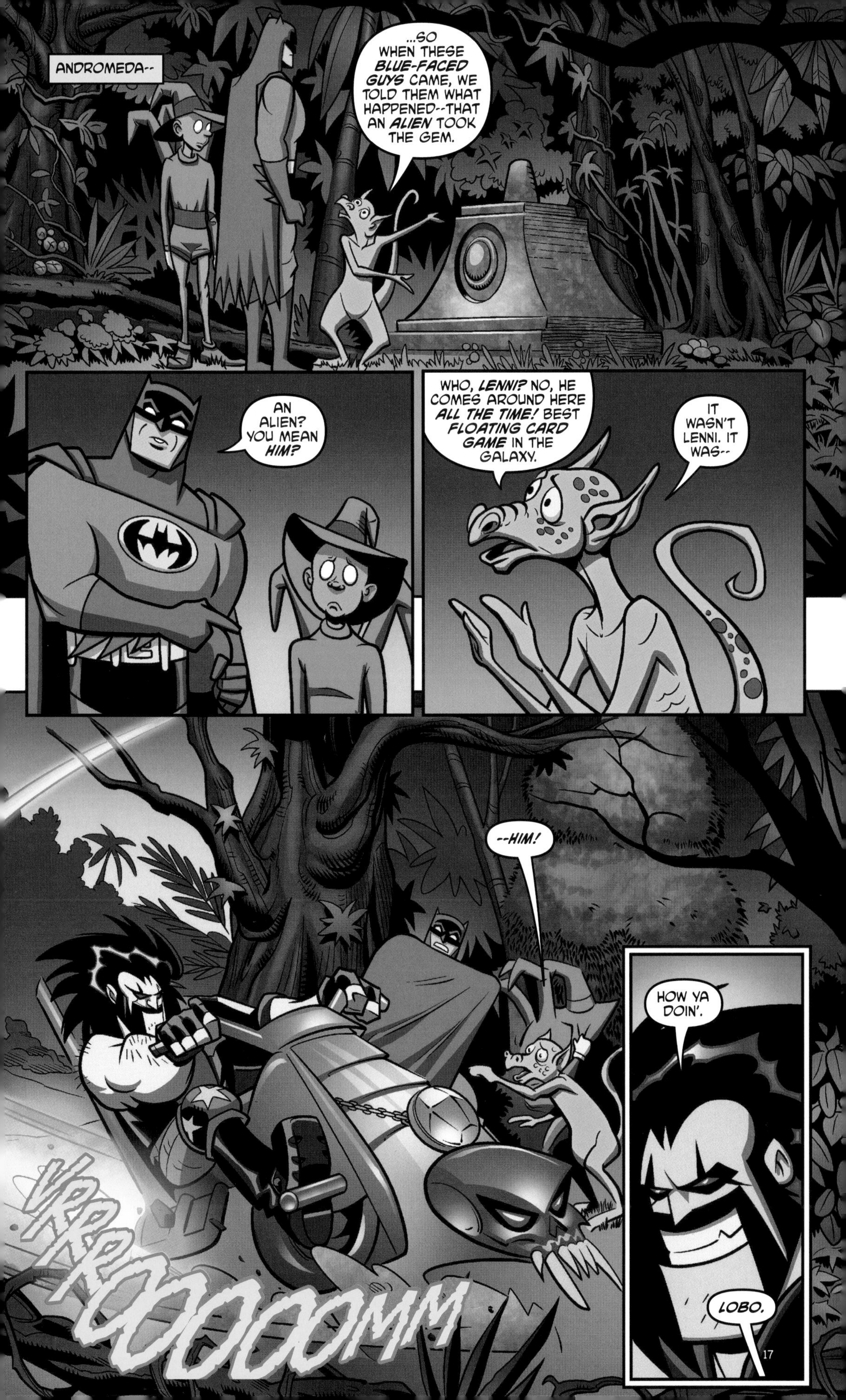

ANDROMEDA--
...SO WHEN THESE BLUE-FACED GUYS CAME, WE TOLD THEM WHAT HAPPENED--THAT AN ALIEN TOOK THE GEM.
AN ALIEN? YOU MEAN HIM?
WHO, LENNI? NO, HE COMES AROUND HERE ALL THE TIME! BEST FLOATING CARD GAME IN THE GALAXY.
IT WASN'T LENNI. IT WAS--
--HIM!
VROOOOOMM
HOW YA DOIN'.
LOBO.

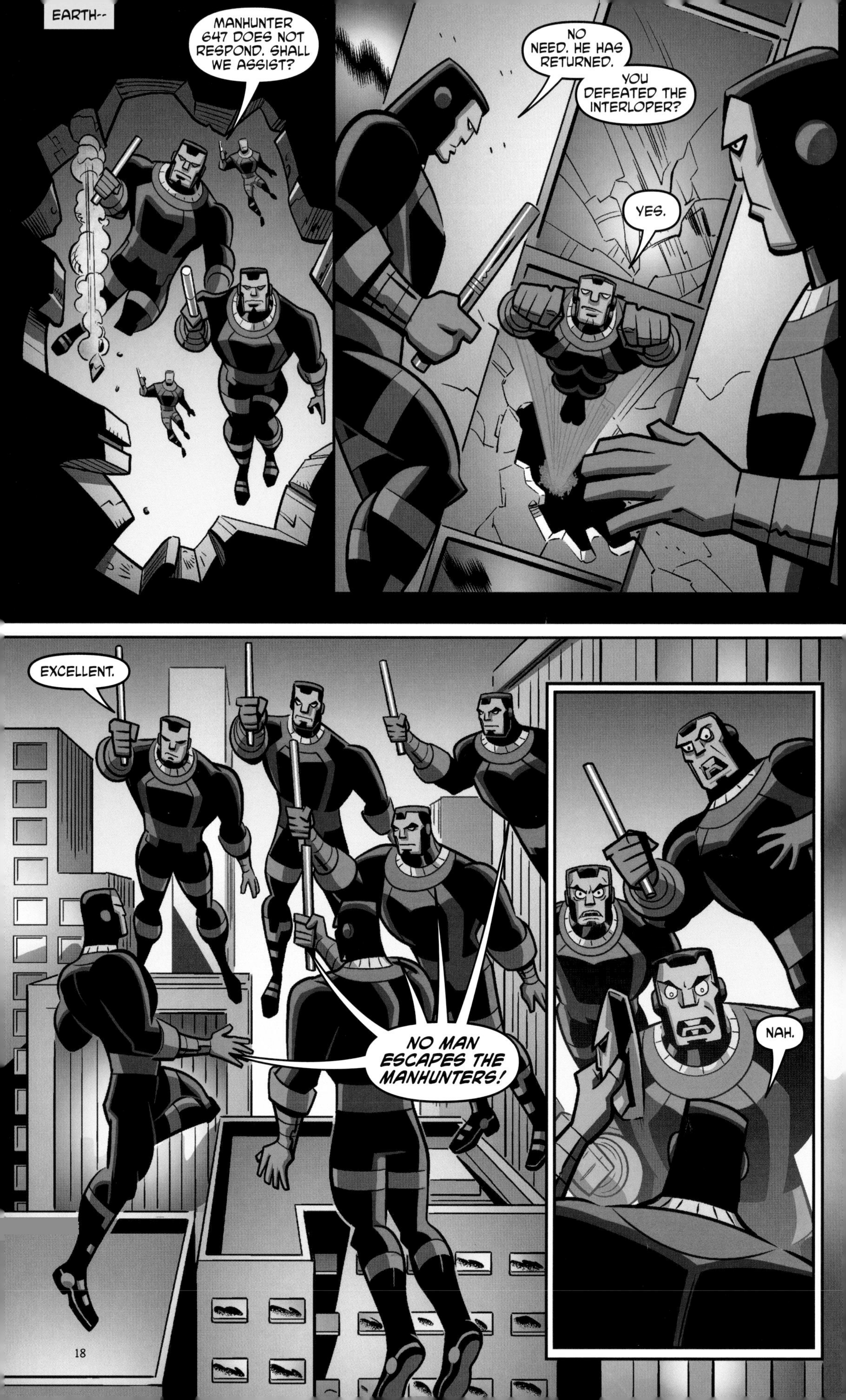
EARTH--
MANHUNTER 647 DOES NOT RESPOND. SHALL WE ASSIST?
NO NEED. HE HAS RETURNED.
YOU DEFEATED THE INTERLOPER?
YES.
EXCELLENT.
NO MAN ESCAPES THE MANHUNTERS!
NAH.

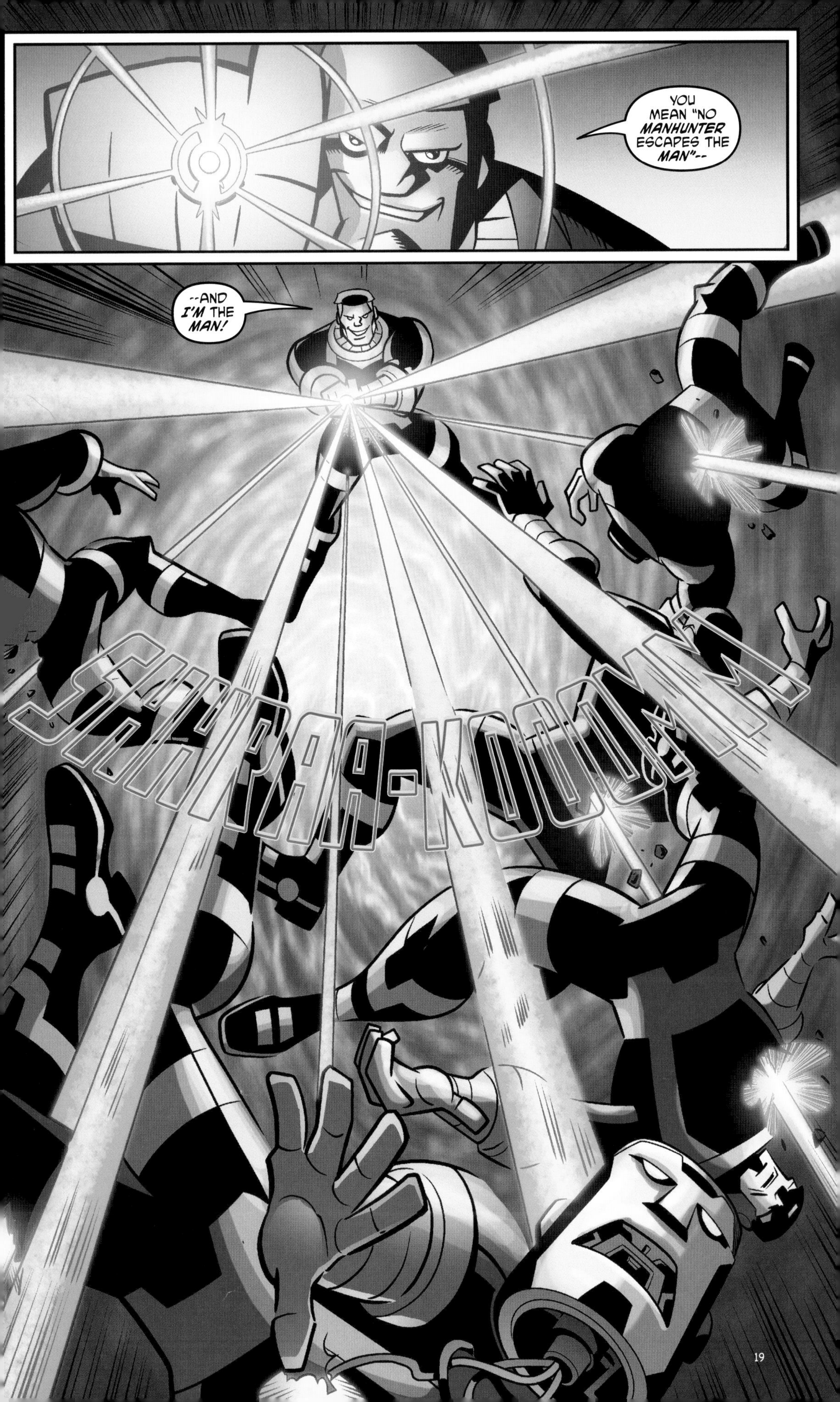
YOU MEAN "NO *MANHUNTER* ESCAPES THE *MAN*"--
--AND *I'M* THE *MAN!*
SHHRAA-KOOOM!

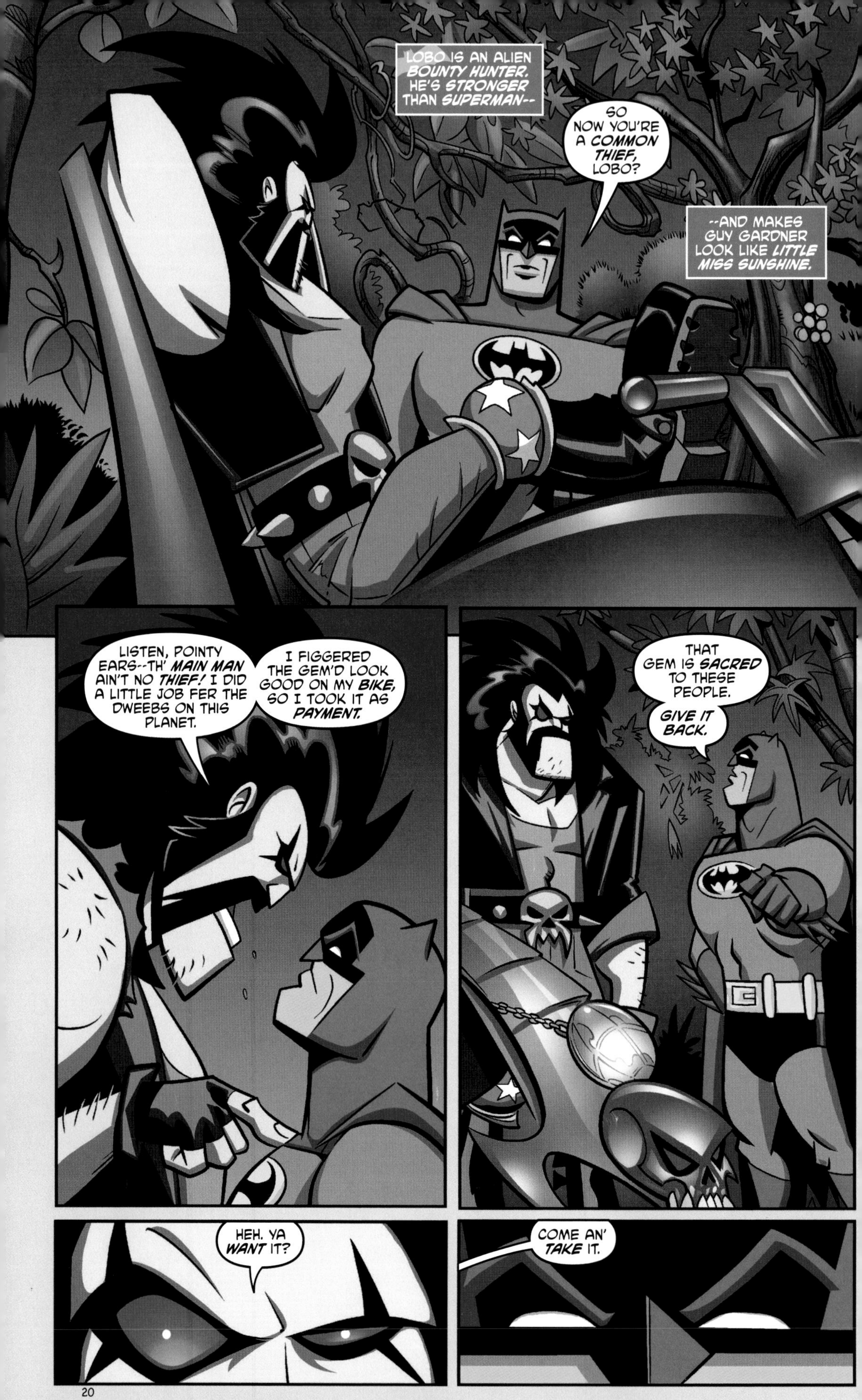
LOBO IS AN ALIEN BOUNTY HUNTER. HE'S STRONGER THAN SUPERMAN--
SO NOW YOU'RE A COMMON THIEF, LOBO?
--AND MAKES GUY GARDNER LOOK LIKE LITTLE MISS SUNSHINE.
LISTEN, POINTY EARS--TH' MAIN MAN AIN'T NO THIEF! I DID A LITTLE JOB FER THE DWEEBS ON THIS PLANET.
I FIGGERED THE GEM'D LOOK GOOD ON MY BIKE, SO I TOOK IT AS PAYMENT.
THAT GEM IS SACRED TO THESE PEOPLE.
GIVE IT BACK.
HEH. YA WANT IT?
COME AN' TAKE IT.

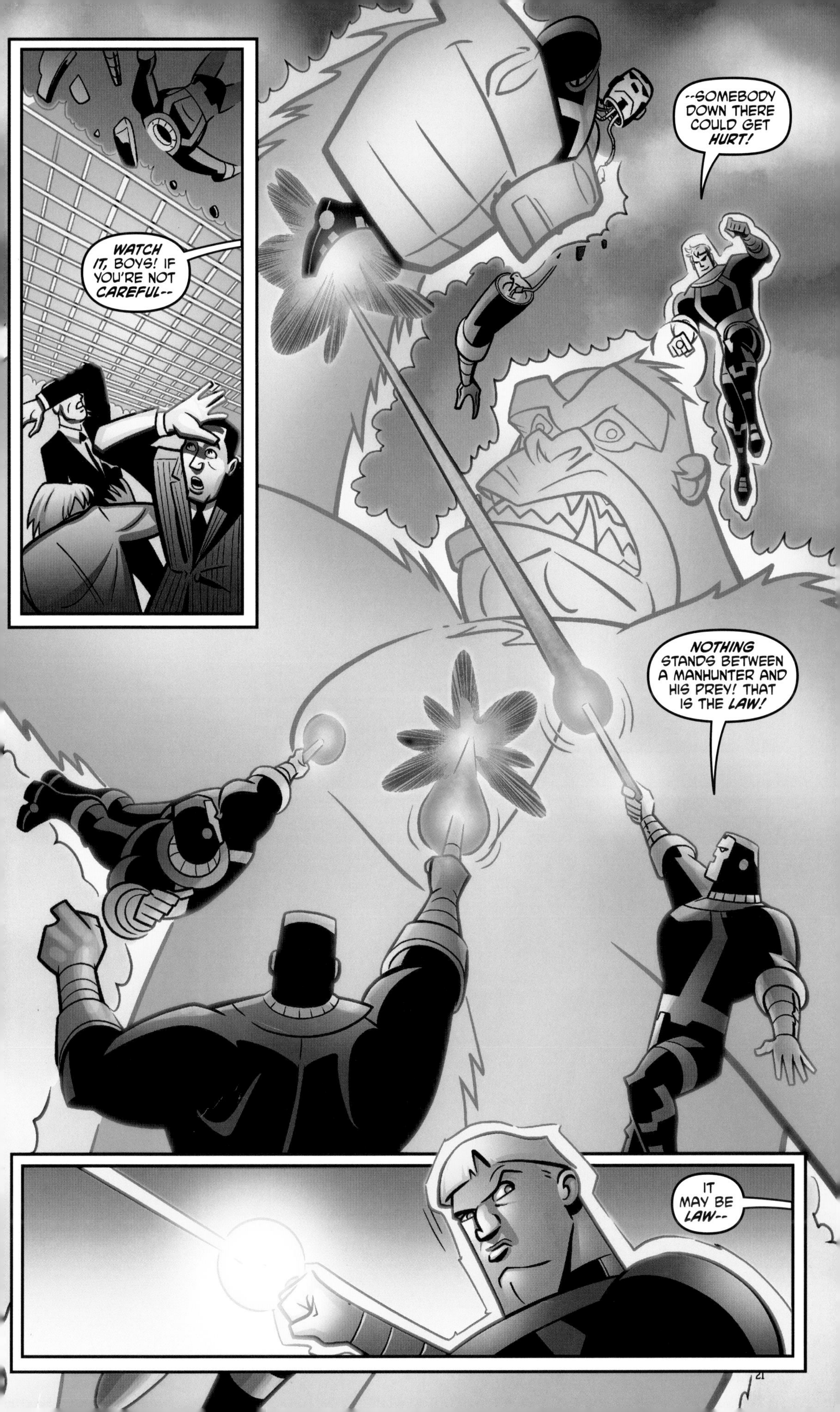
WATCH IT, BOYS! IF YOU'RE NOT CAREFUL--
--SOMEBODY DOWN THERE COULD GET HURT!
NOTHING STANDS BETWEEN A MANHUNTER AND HIS PREY! THAT IS THE LAW!
IT MAY BE LAW--

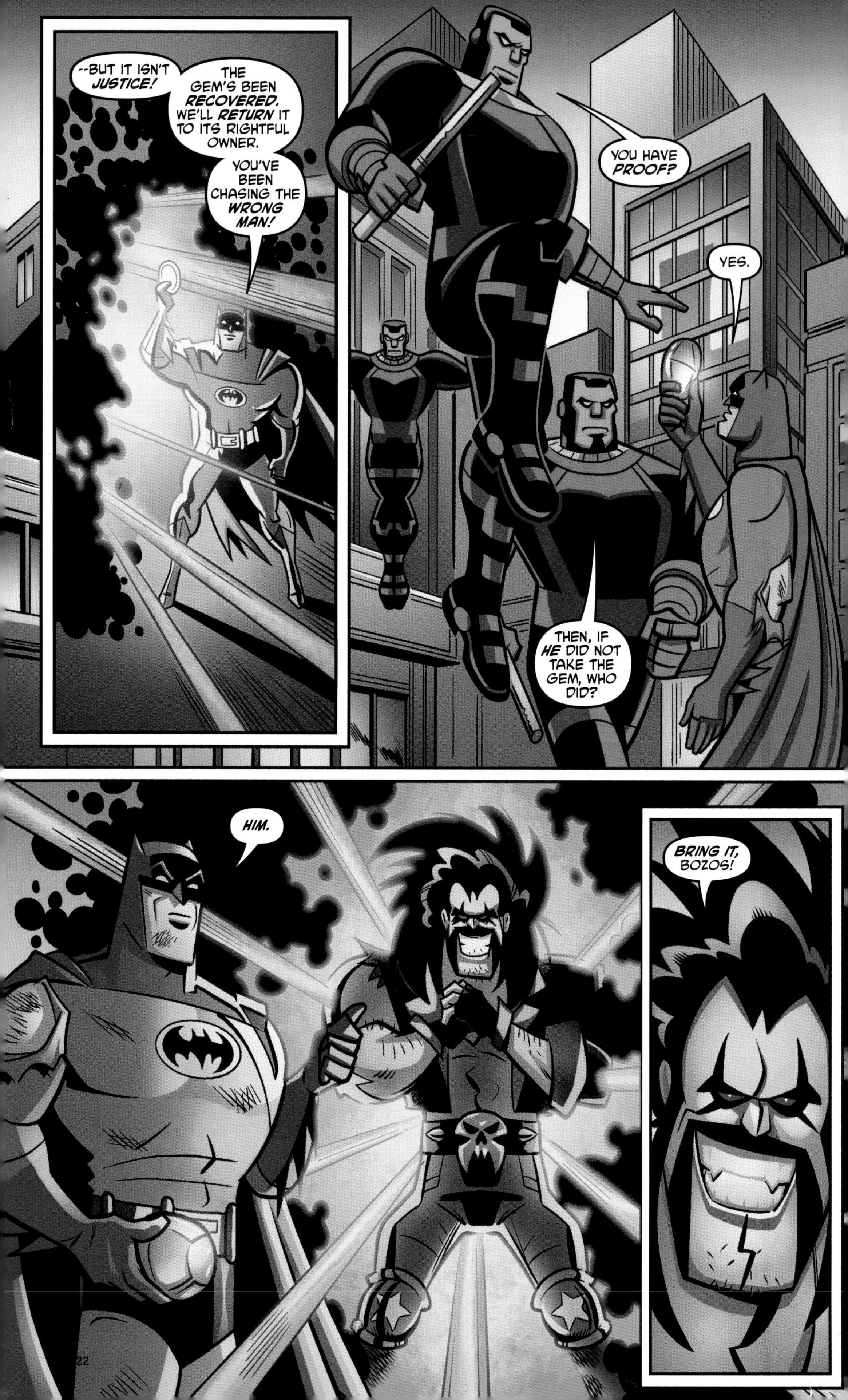
--BUT IT ISN'T JUSTICE!
THE GEM'S BEEN RECOVERED. WE'LL RETURN IT TO ITS RIGHTFUL OWNER.
YOU'VE BEEN CHASING THE WRONG MAN!
YOU HAVE PROOF?
YES.
THEN, IF HE DID NOT TAKE THE GEM, WHO DID?
HIM.
BRING IT, BOZOS!

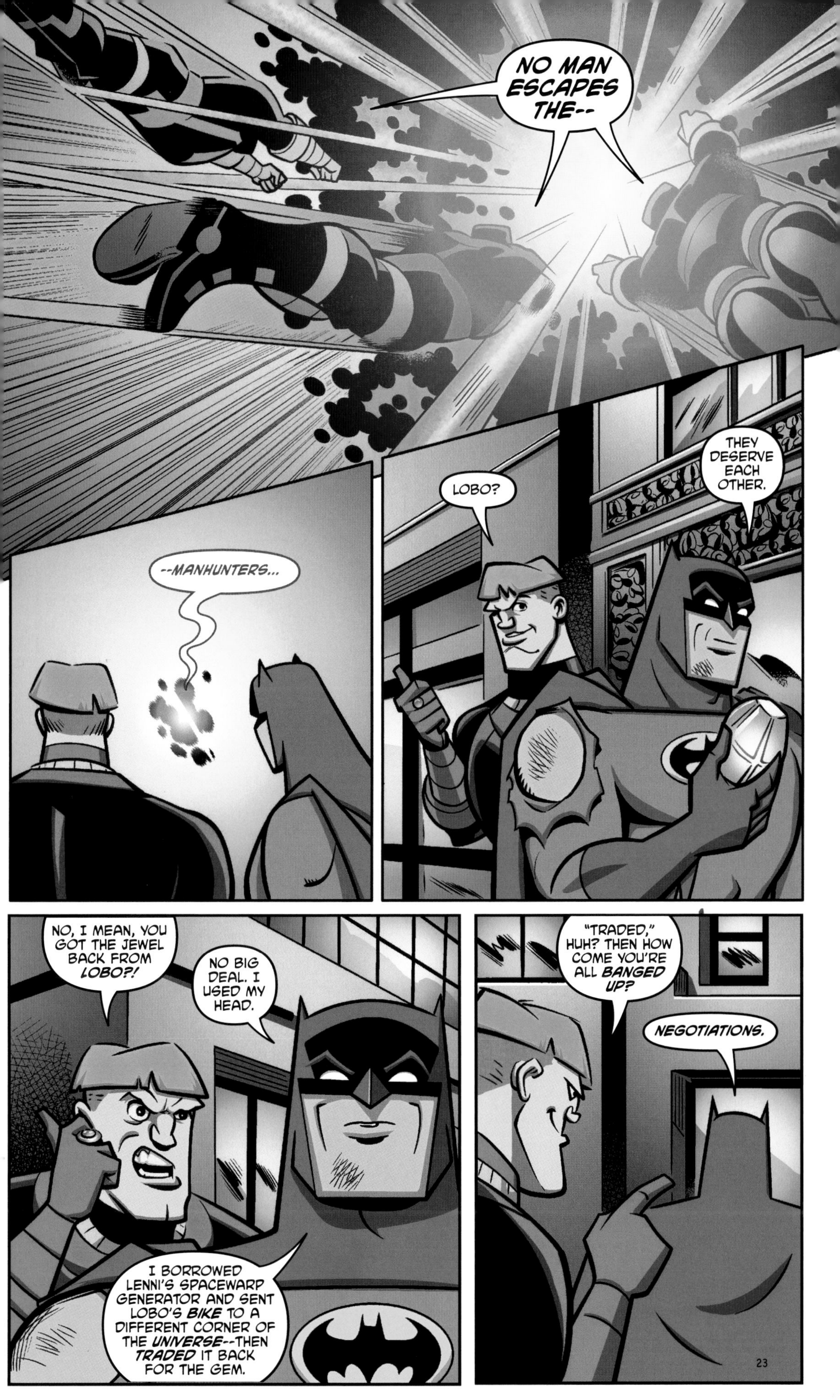

NO MAN ESCAPES THE--
--MANHUNTERS...
LOBO?
THEY DESERVE EACH OTHER.
NO, I MEAN, YOU GOT THE JEWEL BACK FROM *LOBO?!*
NO BIG DEAL. I USED MY HEAD.
I BORROWED LENNI'S SPACEWARP GENERATOR AND SENT LOBO'S *BIKE* TO A DIFFERENT CORNER OF THE *UNIVERSE*--THEN *TRADED* IT BACK FOR THE GEM.
"TRADED," HUH? THEN HOW COME YOU'RE ALL *BANGED UP?*
NEGOTIATIONS.

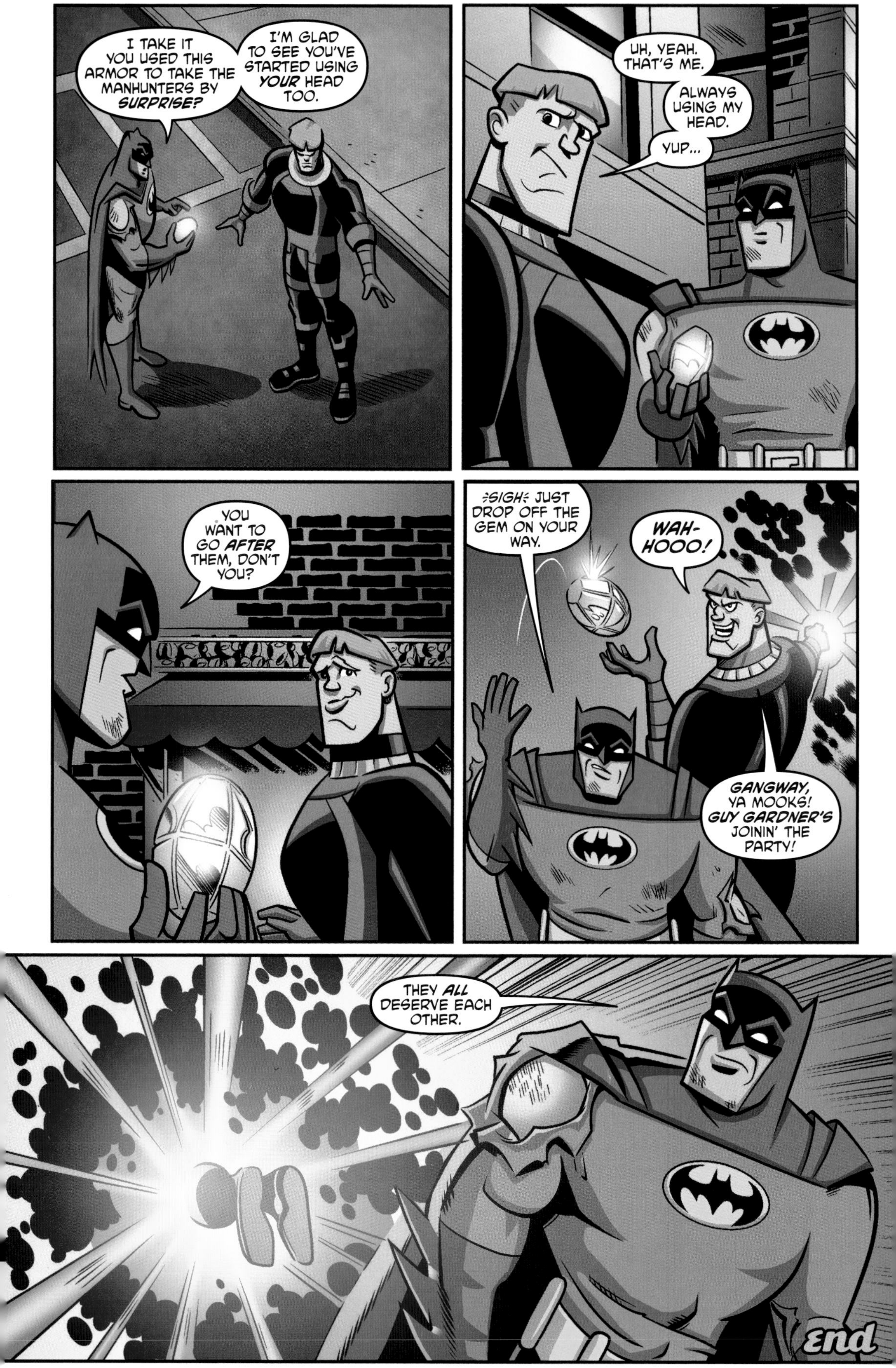

I TAKE IT YOU USED THIS ARMOR TO TAKE THE MANHUNTERS BY SURPRISE?
I'M GLAD TO SEE YOU'VE STARTED USING YOUR HEAD TOO.
UH, YEAH. THAT'S ME.
ALWAYS USING MY HEAD.
YUP...
YOU WANT TO GO AFTER THEM, DON'T YOU?
SIGH JUST DROP OFF THE GEM ON YOUR WAY.
WAH-HOOO!
GANGWAY, YA MOOKS! GUY GARDNER'S JOININ' THE PARTY!
THEY ALL DESERVE EACH OTHER.
End

CREATORS

SHOLLY FISCH
WRITER

Bitten by a radioactive typewriter, Sholly Fisch has spent the wee hours writing books, comics, TV scripts, and online material for over 25 years. His comic book credits include more than 200 stories and features about characters such as Batman, Superman, Bugs Bunny, Daffy Duck, Spider-Man, and Ben 10. Currently, he writes stories for Action Comics every month, plus stories for Looney Tunes and Scooby-Doo. By day, Sholly is a mild-mannered developmental psychologist who helps to create educational TV shows, websites, and other media for kids.

RICK BURCHETT
PENCILLER

Rick Burchett has worked as a comics artist for over 25 years. He has received the comics industry's Eisner Award three times, Spain's Haxtur Award, and he has been nominated for England's Eagle Award. Rick lives with his wife and two sons near St. Louis, Missouri.

DAN DAVIS
INKER

Dan Davis has illustrated the Garfield comic series as well as books for Warner Bros. and DC Comics. He has brought a variety of comic book characters to life, including Batman and the rest of the Super Friends! In 2012, Dan was nominated for an Eisner Award for the Batman: The Brave and the Bold series. He currently resides in Gotham City.

GLOSSARY

assist [uh·SIST]--to help someone and give support

bounty hunter [BOUN·tee HUHN·ter]--a person who brings in other people, usually criminals, for a reward

corps [KOR]--a group of people acting together or a military organization

deserve [di·ZURV]--to be worthy of something based on what you did; to earn

interloper [IN·ter·loh·per]--a person who isn't welcome and meddles in other people's business

negotiation [ni·goh·shee·AY·shuhn]--the act of talking with someone to try to reach an agreement

prey [PRAY]--a person or thing that is being hunted

recover [ri·KUHV·ur]--to get back something that was lost or stolen

restore [ri·STOR]--to bring back to the original condition

sacred [SAY·krid]--holy; something that's very important and should be treated with respect

threaten [THRET·uhn]--to put in danger or to cause trouble

VISUAL QUESTIONS & PROMPTS

1. Why do you think the artists chose to illustrate many Manhunters in this picture instead of just one? What effect does it have on you as you read?

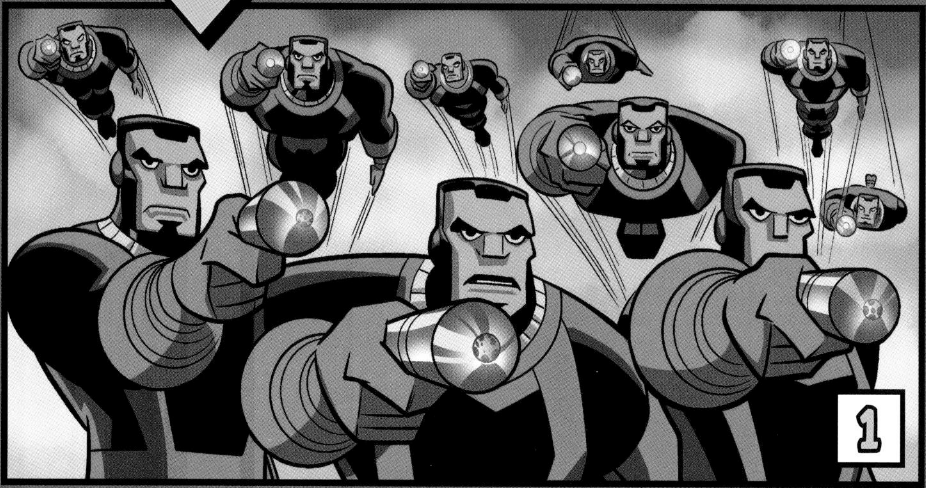
1

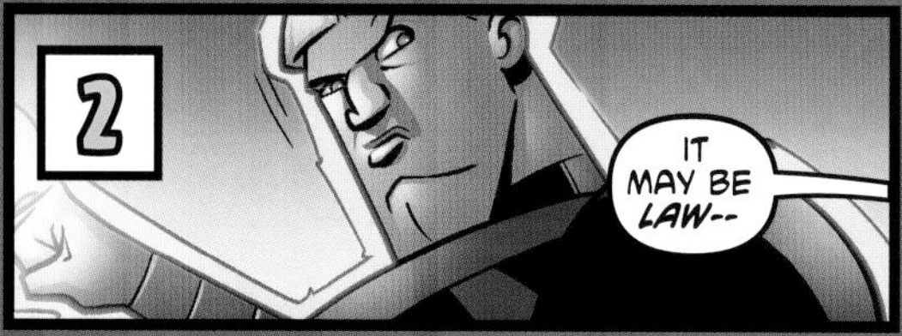
2
IT MAY BE LAW--

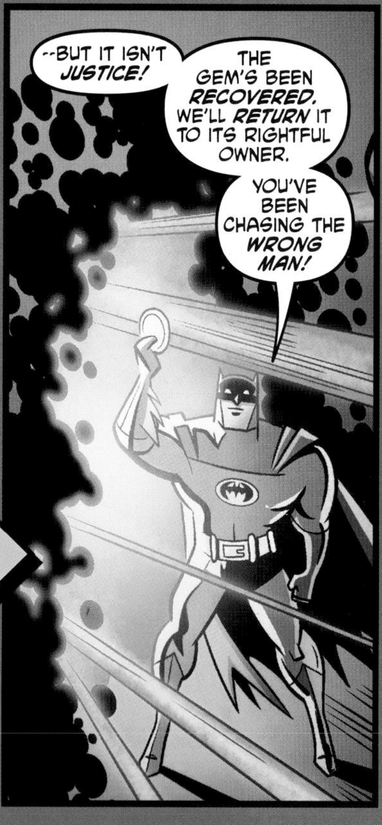
--BUT IT ISN'T JUSTICE!
THE GEM'S BEEN RECOVERED. WE'LL RETURN IT TO ITS RIGHTFUL OWNER.
YOU'VE BEEN CHASING THE WRONG MAN!

2. When Batman says, "It may be law -- but it isn't justice!" what does he mean?

--MANHUNTERS...
3

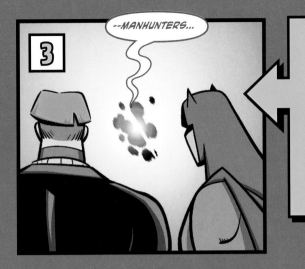

3. We know that the Manhunters left because we can see a disturbance far off in the sky. How else could the artists have depicted this scene?

4. If this panel didn't indicate that Batman and Lenni were in the Andromeda Galaxy, would you be able to tell that they were not on Earth? Why or why not?

THE ANDROMEDA GALAXY--
...GETTING AROUND THE UNIVERSE GOT A LOT EASIER AFTER I WON THIS *SPACEWARP GIZMO* IN A CARD GAME. SO NOW I--
AAAAHHH!
NOT *ANOTHER* ONE!
4

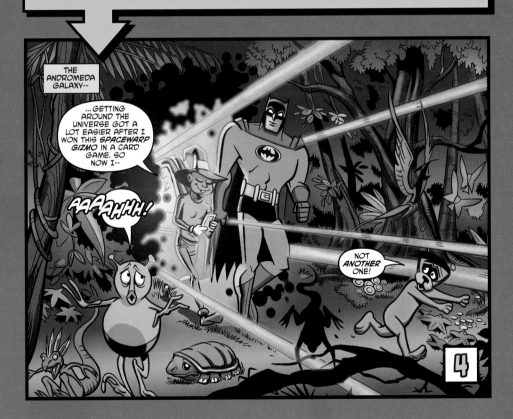

READ THEM ALL!

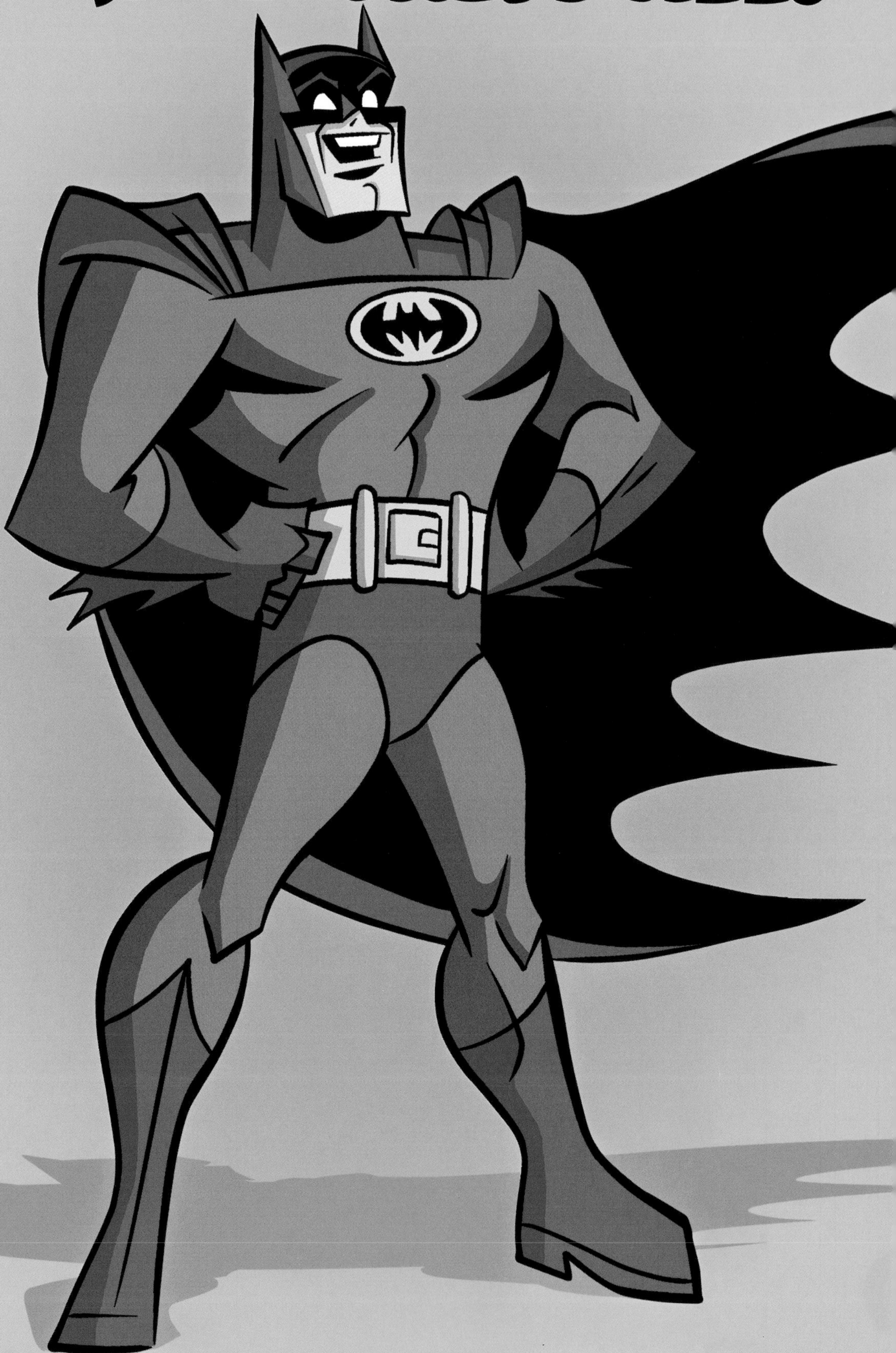

THE ALL NEW!

BATMAN

THE BRAVE AND THE BOLD

THE ALL NEW!
BATMAN
THE BRAVE AND THE BOLD
BOTTLE OF THE PLANETS
FISCH
BURCHETT
DAVIS

THE ALL NEW!
BATMAN
THE BRAVE AND THE BOLD
THAT HOLIDAY FEELING
FISCH
BURCHETT
DAVIS

THE ALL NEW!
BATMAN
THE BRAVE AND THE BOLD
THROUGH THE LOOKING GLASS
FISCH
BURCHETT
DAVIS

THE ALL NEW!
BATMAN
THE BRAVE AND THE BOLD
FISCH
BURCHETT
DAVIS
THE BRIDE AND THE BOLD

THE ALL NEW!
BATMAN
THE BRAVE AND THE BOLD
FISCH
BURCHETT
DAVIS
MANHANDLED BY MANHUNTERS!

THE ALL NEW!
BATMAN
THE BRAVE AND THE BOLD
FISCH
BURCHETT
DAVIS
CLOBBERED BY CLAYFACE!

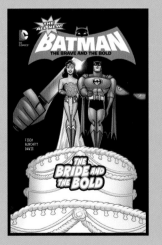

THE ALL NEW!

BATMAN

THE BRAVE AND THE BOLD

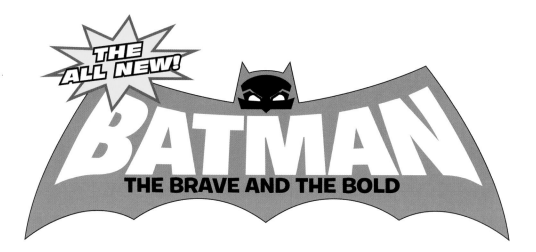